For information address Disney Press,
1101 Flower Street, Glendale, California 91201.

ISBN 978-1-4847-2084-4
T425-2382-5-14223
Printed in China
First Edition
1 3 5 7 9 10 8 6 4 2

For more Disney Press fun, visit www.disneybooks.com
This book was printed on paper created from a sustainable source.

GOOFY'S
SLEDDING CONTEST

BOOK SEVEN

DISNEP PRESS

New York • Los Angeles

One chilly morning, Goofy woke up to find snow outside his window.

"Yahoo!" he yelled. "Winter is here!"

Goofy jumped out of bed and got dressed. Winter was his favorite time of year. He loved getting bundled up in his warmest clothes.

He loved building snowmen and the crunch the snow made as he walked through it.

But most of all, Goofy loved sledding!

Goofy looked at his sleds. They were all fun to ride. But he wondered if there was a faster way down the hill. Goofy went back inside and dug through his closet. He was looking for something that would be slippery enough. Finally, he found just the thing.

His surfboard!

Goofy ran outside and up a hill. He put the surfboard on
the ground, jumped on it, and . . .

. . . sank!

The surfboard was too heavy!

"Gosh," said Goofy. "I guess I need to find something different."

Goofy thought and thought. Then he had an idea.

Goofy got two bananas. He put the peels on his feet and took a step forward.

Bam! Goofy slipped on the peels and fell backward into the snow.

Just then, Mickey came along.

"Why are you lying in the snow?" he asked Goofy.

"I was trying to find the fastest way down the hill," Goofy explained. "I guess I slip on banana peels, but they don't slip on snow!"

"Hmmm," Mickey said. "I have a racing sled. You could borrow that."

"Thanks, Mickey," Goofy said. "I wonder if your sled is faster than mine. Hey, how about a race?"

Goofy was so excited about the idea of a race that he decided to invite all his friends. He called Minnie. Then Minnie called Daisy, and Daisy called Donald.

The friends agreed to meet at the big hill.

But Goofy was still determined to find the fastest way down the hill. He tried and tried to find something faster than a sled, but nothing worked. Maybe a sled was best, after all.

But which sled should Goofy bring?

Goofy looked at all his sleds. Then he piled them into a laundry basket and dragged them up the hill. He would decide what to use later.

When Goofy arrived, Minnie and Daisy were making
a snowman.

"He can judge the race!" said Minnie.

Mickey and Donald were having a snowball fight.

"Hi, Goofy," Donald said, peeking out from behind a tree.

Smack! He was hit by Mickey's snowball.

At the top of the hill, the friends got ready to race. Goofy took his sleds out of his basket. It was time to pick one.

"Everybody ready?" Mickey said. "On your marks, get set . . ."

But Goofy wasn't ready. He turned to ask Mickey to wait . . .

. . . and fell into his laundry basket!

"Go!" yelled Mickey.

"Whoops!" yelled Goofy. The race had started without him.

Just then, the basket started slipping down the hill. It moved faster and faster.

Goofy looked around. He was in the lead! His ears blew back in the wind. Snow flew up all around him.

"Yahoo!" he yelled. He raced past the snowman at the bottom of the hill.

Goofy had won the race!

"You were so fast!" Mickey said.

"How did you think of using a laundry basket?" asked Minnie.

Goofy smiled. "I guess you could say I just stumbled into it!"